FAMILY ISSUES AND YOU™

LIVING WITH AN ILLNESS IN THE FAMILY

VIOLA JONES AND TABITHA WAINWRIGHT

rosen publishing's
rosen central®
NEW YORK

Published in 2016 by The Rosen Publishing Group, Inc.
29 East 21st Street, New York, NY 10010

Copyright © 2016 by The Rosen Publishing Group, Inc.

First Edition

All rights reserved. No part of this book may be reproduced in any form without permission in writing from the publisher, except by a reviewer.

Library of Congress Cataloging-in-Publication Data

Jones, Viola.
 Living with an illness in the family / Viola Jones and Tabitha Wainwright. – First edition.
     pages cm. – (Family issues and you)
 Audience: Grades 5-8.
 Includes index.
 ISBN 978-1-4994-3693-8 (library bound) – ISBN 978-1-4994-3694-5 (pbk.) – ISBN 978-1-4994-3695-2 (6-pack)
 1. Sick–Family relationships–Juvenile literature. 2. Families–Health and hygiene–Juvenile literature. I. Wainwright, Tabitha. II. Title.
 R726.5.J66 2016
 610–dc23

2015017931

Manufactured in the United States of America

CONTENTS

INTRODUCTION   4

CHAPTER ONE
WHAT TO EXPECT   6

CHAPTER TWO
HOW TO ADAPT TO CHANGES IN YOUR FAMILY   16

CHAPTER THREE
DON'T NEGLECT YOURSELF   26

CHAPTER FOUR
WHEN HOPE RUNS OUT   35

GLOSSARY   41
FOR MORE INFORMATION   42
FOR FURTHER READING   45
INDEX   46

INTRODUCTION

Being young is supposed to be a fun and carefree time. Your biggest problem is the test you have on Thursday. Mostly, it's having fun with friends, playing sports, watching television, reading books, and whatever else you want to do. When you are this age, the last thing on your mind is serious illness.

But let's say that someone in your family is sick enough that it changes your life. It could be your mom or dad, a grandparent, or your brother or sister. Suddenly, instead of living the carefree life of a young person, you're faced with very real problems.

When dealing with illness in your family, whether it's life threatening or temporary, you may experience many new feelings. You may feel scared, worried, stressed, sad, or lonely. You may have to take on extra responsibilities and may have to adjust your schedule to meet the needs of your family. If your mother usually drives you to soccer practice and she is in the hospital, you will have to see if you can get a ride with a friend. If you live in a single-parent family and your father is bedridden with pneumonia, you and your siblings will have to prepare your own meals.

When a family member is sick, trying to figure out how to go about your day-to-day life can be very challenging. Although reading about this subject cannot

INTRODUCTION | 5

Having a sick parent can affect your life in ways you might not have imagined. Working together as a family can help smooth out the difficult times.

make a sick person better, it can provide you with useful information that will help you understand what you are feeling. It can also teach you how to cope with these tough situations. Having a sick relative affects your life, but it doesn't have to mean that you have no life.

CHAPTER ONE

WHAT TO EXPECT

You never know how you're going to deal with a stressful situation until it arises. No one expects to have to deal with a family illness, so it is not something most of us prepare for. Whether it's your mom, brother, uncle—or even your dog—who falls ill, it is helpful to think in advance about how you would handle it. Knowing what to expect can help you adapt to the new situation in your family. Some illnesses happen suddenly, while others present themselves gradually. Each has its own challenges.

WHEN YOU'RE TAKEN BY SURPRISE

When an illness shows itself suddenly—like a heart attack—it can be more of a shock than an illness that progresses slowly. One minute you're going about your daily routine and the next minute, your life has changed dramatically.

It was Theo's birthday, and all he could think about was the big party his mom was throwing him after school. All his friends were coming over to play games and eat cake. Theo couldn't wait to get home to help his mom decorate and see how many presents she had bought him. When he finally turned the corner, he saw an ambulance with flashing red lights in his driveway. Confused, Theo ran over to the ambulance. The first person he saw was Marcia, his mom's best friend from next door. When Marcia saw Theo, she took him aside and told him that his mom had had a heart attack and would have to stay in the hospital for a while. Since Theo didn't have any family close-by, he would have to stay next door with Marcia until his mother could come home.

Theo's mother's sudden illness—she had a heart attack and her left side was paralyzed—was very startling. After all, his mother had been fine in the morning. Theo couldn't believe it was true, even after he went to the hospital and saw his mother lying pale and weak in bed.

During the first few hospital visits, Theo would talk on and on, telling his mother how he wanted her to come home so that they could finish building a tree house in the backyard. He told his mother that he didn't understand why she was still in the hospital. In fact, Theo seemed completely unaware that his inability to come to terms with the seriousness of his mother's situation was causing his mother stress.

Denial is when you are not able

When your loved one has a serious illness, you may want to research the condition on the Internet. If you understand what your loved one is going through, it will be easier to deal with the situation.

LIVING WITH AN ILLNESS IN THE FAMILY

to accept the reality of a situation. This is a common reaction to a sudden illness. This was Theo's reaction—to deny that his mother's heart attack had even happened. In fact, Theo's mother and Marcia became concerned about Theo, because he was having such a hard time facing reality. On behalf of Theo's mother, Marcia spoke to the hospital social worker, who in turn sat down with Theo and went over a list of emotions that he would probably be experiencing, specifically denial, anger, confusion, fear, and guilt.

TALKING TO SOMEONE ABOUT YOUR FEELINGS

Theo was relieved once he talked with the social worker. He had been very confused by the different feelings that he was experiencing. Richard, the social worker, helped Theo create a chart so that he could keep track of his feelings. The two met once a week and went over the chart. Richard described different emotions, and together they came up with definitions for the emotions. Then Theo would fill in the columns with the name of the emotion that related to how he was feeling.

After his weekly session with Richard, Theo felt a hundred times better. He felt less confused and afraid, and he knew the reasons why he felt the way he felt. This is why it is very important to share your feelings. If you have a sick family member and you need to talk to someone, try talking to an older

WHAT TO EXPECT | 9

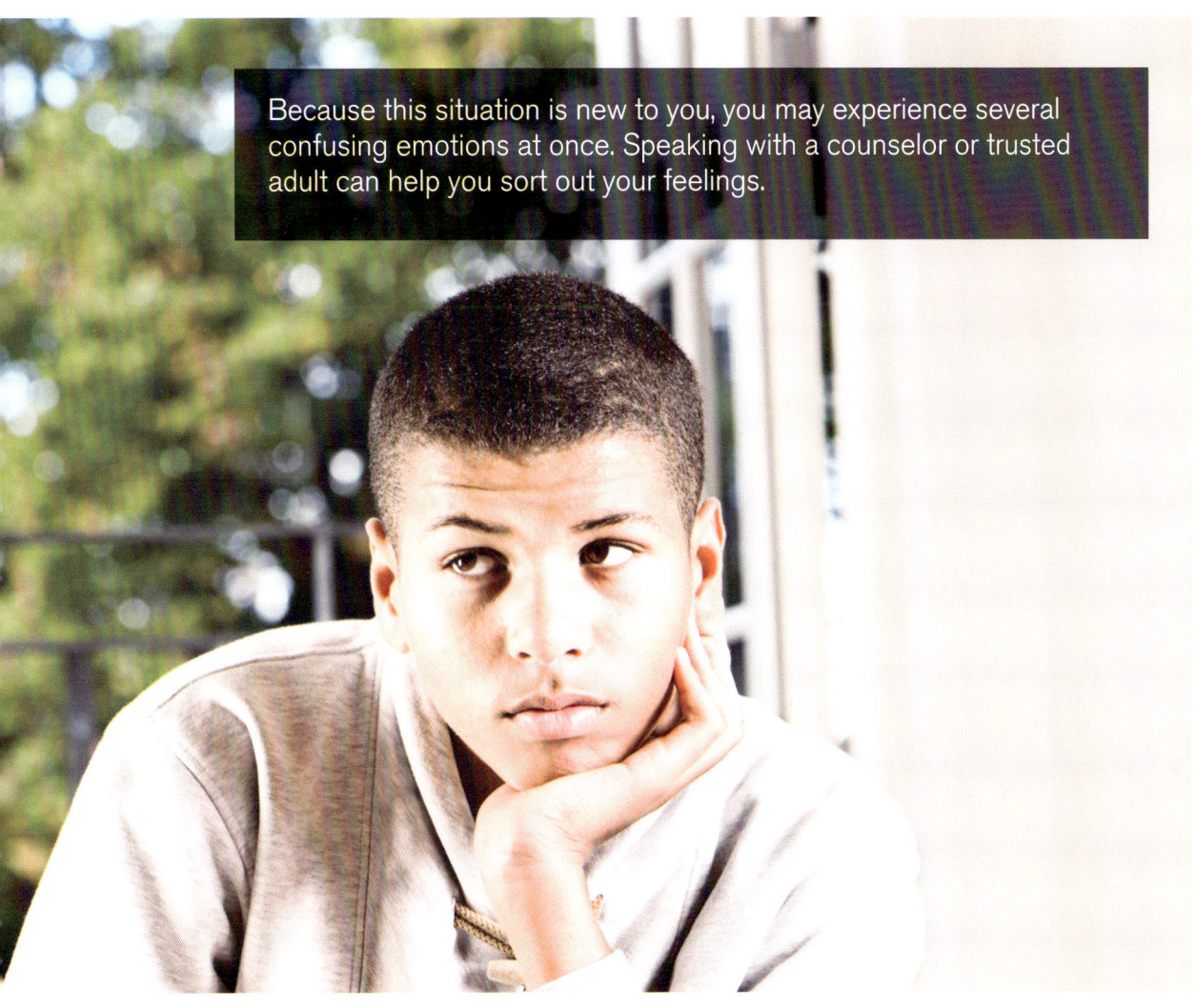

Because this situation is new to you, you may experience several confusing emotions at once. Speaking with a counselor or trusted adult can help you sort out your feelings.

brother or sister, a close neighbor, another relative, or a teacher or counselor at school, or ask an older relative to contact a hotline or social worker with whom you can speak.

IT'S OK TO FEEL ANGRY ... AND SAD

It is important to understand that it is all right to experience a variety of confusing feelings. Even anger is a natural reaction to

LIVING WITH AN ILLNESS IN THE FAMILY

this kind of stressful situation. Don't feel guilty or mad at yourself if you are annoyed at your sick family member, or if you are mad because you are getting less attention than you usually do. Instead, allow yourself to feel angry (at least for a little while), and let someone who is close to you know that you are feeling this way. Once you acknowledge your emotions, you will feel better.

If you feel sad or lonely and you want to cry, don't be afraid that doing so will mean that you are weak. Crying is good for us. It allows us to release some of what we are feeling. Once you start expressing your emotions, and you let other people close to you know how you are feeling, it will be easier to move to the final step of dealing with an illness—acceptance.

KEEPING TRACK OF YOUR EMOTIONS

Writing down your emotions when you have them can help you make sense of how you're feeling during this difficult time. Being forced to understand how you feel can help you deal with it better. Remember to be honest. No one has to see this but you. Here is an example of an emotion diary you might create in the course of a week.

Emotion: Denial
Definition: Inability to believe what is going on.

What I feel: I can't believe Mom is sick. It just can't be true. I don't get it. Maybe when I go back to the hospital tomorrow, she'll be fine.

Emotion: Anger
Definition: Being mad at the way things are.
What I feel: I'm mad that Mom is in the hospital and not at home with me. I'm mad I didn't get my party. I'm mad that Dad doesn't live in this country. I'm mad this is happening.

Emotion: Confusion
Definition: Inability to understand things.
What I feel: Sometimes I feel OK and then other times I feel really sorry for Mom. Sometimes I feel bad that I can go out and play and she has to stay in the hospital. My parents are divorced and Dad lives in France, and I don't know if I should call him since he and Mom don't get along well.

Emotion: Fear
Definition: Being scared; having a funny feeling in your stomach.
What I feel: I want to cry a lot. What if Mom dies? What if I leave the stove on by mistake and I burn down the house? Where will I go?

Emotion: Guilt
Definition: Feeling bad about something.
What I feel: I feel bad that I still want my birthday party. I feel bad that I sometimes wish that my best friend's mother was in the hospital, too, so I wouldn't be alone.

WHEN IT CREEPS UP ON YOU

You may react differently to an illness that develops gradually. You may have a family member who has an illness that is slowly getting worse. If you are in this kind of situation, you may experience an even more confusing variety of emotions, and they may last for a longer period of time.

Manny's sister Alana was born with a heart defect. Since she was a baby, Alana had always been very weak and the whole family had always been extra careful with her. When Alana got a little older, her doctor suggested that she undergo an operation to fix her heart. Since Manny was used to thinking of his sister as "sick," he didn't think much of the news of his sister's surgery. In fact, he didn't even know what it meant.

His parents, on the other hand, were extremely worried, and they become annoyed with Manny for being what they said was "insensitive." For a while, Manny went to his friend Jerry's house every day after school. He needed to get away from his crazy, spoiled sister and his annoying parents.

After he had shown up at Jerry's house five days in a row, Mrs. Soloway, Jerry's mom, asked him if anything was going on at home that he would like to talk about.

"It's awful, Mrs. Soloway. Everyone is being mean to me and it's just because Alana is still sick and may have this heart surgery. They don't seem to care about me anymore at all."

"Manny," replied Mrs. Soloway, "of course they care about you. It's just that Alana is having a serious and scary operation. Didn't anyone tell you what it involves?"

"No," replied Manny.

After that, Manny and Mrs. Soloway, who was a nurse, had a long talk about the surgery and Manny's feelings. Manny felt relieved to know that his family didn't hate him. He now understood that they were just extra worried about Alana, and that he had misunderstood the whole thing. He also realized that just as he was thinking that they no longer cared about him, perhaps his parents and sister were upset that he was spending all of his time at Jerry's house.

Manny didn't stay at Jerry's house for dinner that night. He quickly went home to give his parents and sister a hug.

Manny's anger and confusion at how his family was reacting was due to the lack of information that was communicated to him about what was going on with his sister. Manny had not asked any questions and no one had taken the time to discuss the surgery with him. At this point, if Manny were to have written a list of what he was feeling, it would have included the following:

- Anger
- Annoyance
- Frustration
- Betrayal
- Sadness
- Confusion
- Loneliness

That's a lot of emotions for one person. And a lot of them could have been avoided if Manny's family had worked more at communicating their feelings and explaining what Alana was going through.

DO THE RESEARCH

When you find out that a family member is sick, you may want to have more of an understanding of what that person is going

LIVING WITH AN ILLNESS IN THE FAMILY

through. If a parent decides to shield you from the severity—or seriousness—of a situation, that is his or her choice. But you should feel free to ask questions.

Since doing research on your own can be confusing, and since inaccurate information is easy to come by if you look in the wrong places (some Internet sites post unauthorized information, for example), try asking a teacher, librarian, or older relative to direct you to good sources of information.

Knowledge can be powerful. If you have an understanding of what someone with an illness is going through, you will be better equipped to cope effectively with the situation. Not only

A professional counselor can help your family learn to communicate with each other. During an illness, emotions are high and everyone's priorities change, but it is important to communicate with one another.

will you know what to expect, but you will also be aware of how you can help the ill person in your family.

In general, communication is an important part of all family matters, but it is especially vital in times of crisis, such as when a family member is ill. Communication involves conveying your feelings—and your fears—to your family so that you can all be sources of support for one another. It also means understanding as much as you can about the illness and its impact on your sick relative. Unfortunately, during such emotional and stressful times, you may find that it is harder than usual to communicate with your family members. This is surely a difficult time for everyone involved. If you are having trouble communicating with a parent, sibling, or other family member, you may want to find someone outside of the family—such as a school counselor—who will listen and help you sort through your emotions. It is important not to keep your feelings and your fears to yourself.

Chapter Two

HOW TO ADAPT TO CHANGES IN YOUR FAMILY

Confusing emotions are not the only changes brought on by an illness in your family. Your life might change in many other ways. You may find your daily routine affected. You will possibly be asked to do things around the house that you never had to do before. You may be given new and important responsibilities. All of these changes can leave you lost and confused and missing your old life.

CHANNEL YOUR FRUSTRATION INTO SOMETHING PRODUCTIVE

With an ill family member at home or in the hospital, it is very likely that you may have less free time. This will especially be true if you live in a single-parent home, if you do not have any other siblings, or—in the case of a more serious illness—if most of your extended family members live far away.

Your first reaction to being told that you can't go out, or that you must come right home from school, will probably be anger. However, no matter how annoyed you feel, it is important that you also realize that now, more than ever, your family really needs your help. As we discussed earlier, it's natural to feel angry, but it's what you do with that anger that is important.

HOW TO ADAPT TO CHANGES IN YOUR FAMILY | 17

When someone in your family is ill, you may be asked to take on more responsibilities. This can mean that you don't have time to play with the other kids in the neighborhood.

In this kind of situation, put your anger to work for you. When people become annoyed, they often get a rush of energy called adrenaline. Use this adrenaline rush to help clean up the dishes, water the plants, pick up your younger brother from school, or make a nice card for whoever is in the hospital.

THERE IS NO SHAME IN NEEDING HELP

Your family situation may be such that with one parent ill and the other working long hours, you and your brothers and sisters will have to take on a lot of extra work around the house. Perhaps you are an only child. Or maybe you live in a single-parent home and you have no other siblings or relatives who are close-by. Families come in all sorts of sizes, and however your particular family is constructed, you may find yourself in a bind.

If this is the case, you may want to see if you can arrange for another relative or family friend to give you some help. If no one is available, ask a neighbor. It is important to remember that it is not bad or a sign of weakness to ask for help. Some people find it very difficult and embarrassing, especially if you need to ask for help from someone that you don't know very well. In these situations, remember that for the most part, people are a compassionate and caring bunch. Most people are happy to help.

If it still makes you feel uncomfortable to ask a neighbor to drive you to a store or to help you change a lightbulb, you can always offer to reciprocate the favor. You could set up a system by which you keep track of what the neighbor (or friend) has helped you with, and you could suggest doing any of the following for them:

- Mow lawn
- Rake leaves
- Water plants
- Feed and/or walk pets
- Babysit
- Help with grocery shopping
- Return library books
- Wash car

WHEN A PARENT IS SICK: TACKLING THE EXTRA WORK SYSTEMATICALLY

If your mother or father is sick, you may have to pick up the housework and chores that they did every day. If you have a

HOW TO ADAPT TO CHANGES IN YOUR FAMILY | 19

brother or sister who can help you, it's best to divide up these jobs. You may want to write out a schedule and put it somewhere where you can see it easily. If you cooperate with each other and take turns cooking meals or helping to buy groceries, you will still be able to spend time doing the things that you normally do, like hanging out with your friends and riding your bike.

Since doing extra housework is not the most fun thing in the world, and since dividing up the extra tasks may be kind of stressful, you might want to change this process into a fun activity. This way, you will take the emphasis off the negative—

Sharing additional chores with your brother or sister can decrease the stress of having extra work to do. You might also consider splitting up the new responsibilities.

doing more work and deciding who will clean the toilets—and focus on the positive side—working together to make your household run more smoothly.

A good way to divide the tasks is with a Task Hat. You'll need paper, pens, scissors, a coin, a piece of colored cardboard, and a hat. First, make a list of all the tasks that need to be done. Then, cut each piece of paper into fourths and write one task on each slip. Fold the slips and put them into the hat. Next comes the fun part: Flip a coin to see who will pick first from the hat. The first player picks a slip from the Task Hat. Then the second player picks a slip from the hat. This continues until the Task Hat is empty. Open each slip and read what is written on it. If you want to trade tasks, you can. Make a schedule. Write the days of the week on the colored piece of cardboard and write down who will be doing each chore on a particular day. If you do end up making weekly charts, you may want to keep them to show to your ill parent or relative. Your mother or father will be very impressed with your excellent organizational skills. Seeing that things are going well at home will raise their spirits considerably.

WHEN A SIBLING IS SICK: GETTING PAST THE RESENTMENT

If your brother or sister is ill, whether he or she is at home or at the hospital, you may feel different about helping out than you would if a parent were ill. Don't be surprised if you feel angry, resentful, lonely, or frustrated.

First of all, you'll be happy to know that it is not unusual to feel this way. Second of all, it is normal to feel a bit of resentment. Many people experience a different set of emotions

EVERYONE'S DIFFERENT

If your sibling is ill, chances are you will behave differently than if he or she were healthy. Maybe you've always been a straight-A student who follows the rules. The stress from having a sick sibling might make you want to act out and skip school, be disrespectful to your parents, and ignore what's expected of you. Or perhaps you've felt like you were always doing something wrong because your parents scold you a lot, and now you feel guilty because your sibling is ill. Maybe now you try to be the perfect child. You start following the rules and doing everything right, in order to make your parents proud.

Everyone reacts differently to stressful situations. Your parents might be too busy to notice the changes in you—or to deal with them—but it is important to recognize how your emotions are impacting your behavior.

when a brother or sister is sick. This is because you have a very different relationship with your siblings than you do with your parent or parents.

Unlike how you feel about your parent, you may think of your brother or sister as an equal. If he or she is ill and therefore doesn't have to make his or her bed or clean the bathroom, you may feel that you don't need to do these things either. This is where your emotions become more complicated

LIVING WITH AN ILLNESS IN THE FAMILY

and you might find yourself regressing—or reverting back to how you behaved when you were younger. We regress when we feel that our needs are not being met. This is why, although you want to be mature and help out, you may find yourself acting childish, resenting all of the attention that your sick brother or sister is getting.

Just to prove that regression is normal and that you are not the only one who feels jealous or left out, take a look at the quotes below. These quotes come from kids who were asked how they felt when they had a sick brother or sister.

> When I was ten, my little sister broke both her legs in a skiing accident. Every day, people came over to sign her casts. She was allowed to talk on the phone and play video games way more than I was. In fact, I never had time to play since I had to water all of the plants and help Mom cook dinner.
>
> I felt really bad until I talked to my aunt. She told me that my mom felt responsible for my sister's accident. After that, I realized that my mom was really worried about my sister. I guess my childish behavior wasn't helping.
>
> My aunt told Mom how I was feeling, and the next day Mom gave me a hug as soon as I came home from school. She told me she was really glad I was around to help her. She said that when my sister got better, she was going to take me to an Orioles game to thank me for doing so much stuff around the house.
> —John, thirteen, Baltimore, MD
>
> My brother was in the hospital for a year because his school bus was in an accident and he was in a coma for

a long time. I felt bad for him but I was mad our friends would call the house and ask how he was doing before they would ask to speak to me. The worst was when a girl at school who I really like, asked if she could go visit him! It was as if no one knew I even existed. I felt really awful and I even stopped doing my homework since my teachers didn't seem to care. I didn't even go to the hospital to see my brother since just thinking of him made me mad.

 After I moped around the house for a few weeks, my dad asked me what was wrong. He had assumed that I was worried about my brother but I told him that I felt like everyone liked him better than me and I was the one who should have been in the coma. Dad looked really surprised to hear me say all of that. He explained that people were really concerned about my brother and that it wasn't a question of people liking him better. After that, I started to go to the hospital every other day to visit.

    —Ramiz, eleven, Baton Rouge, LA

 While it is OK to regress for a while, now is the time when your parents will really need to count on you. Let them know how you feel, and then remind yourself that being sick isn't a treat. Your sick sibling isn't having any fun with chicken pox or pneumonia. If you are feeling that you are doing all sorts of extra work and no one is paying any attention to you, don't be afraid to let your parents know how you are feeling.

 If you don't feel comfortable telling your parents that you are feeling left out, try writing a note. Some people find it easier to express themselves in writing. A simple "I miss you"

24 | LIVING WITH AN ILLNESS IN THE FAMILY

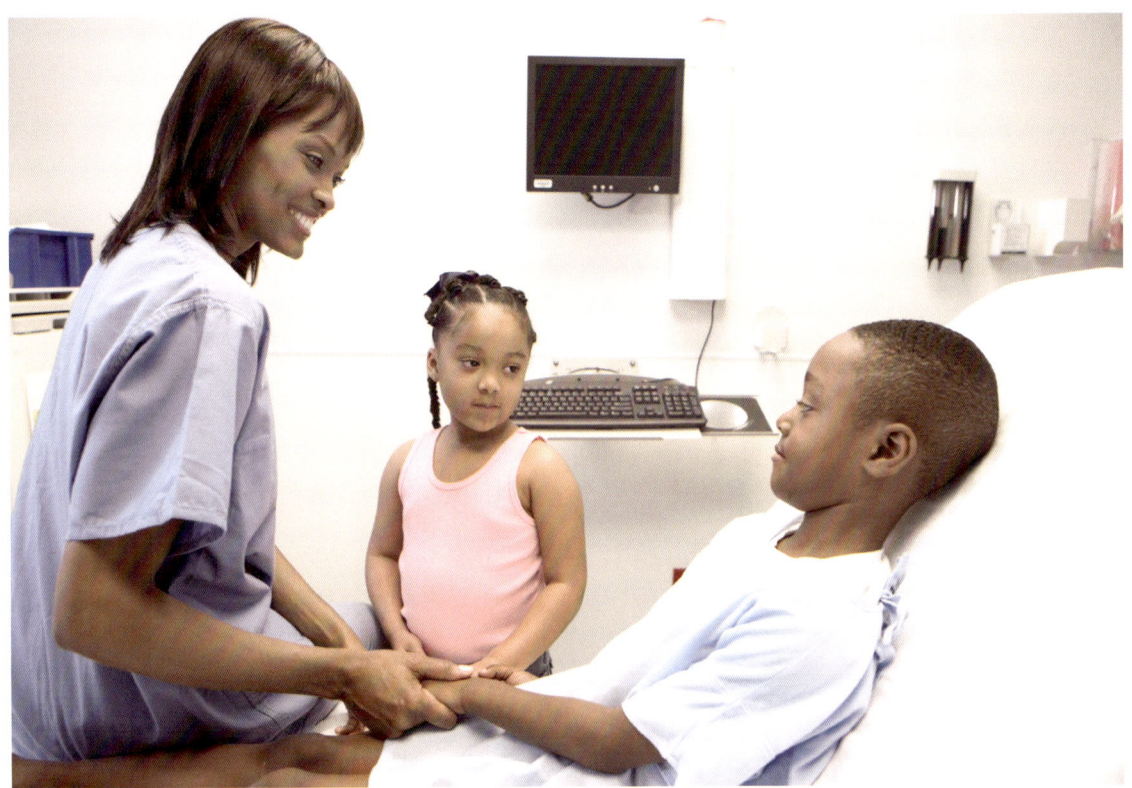

The absence of a sibling can throw off the balance of your family. For instance, if your older brother is sick, you may find yourself suddenly having to figure things out on your own.

or "Mom, I wish I could see more of you" can do a lot. Or tell another relative or family friend how you are feeling. Maybe he or she could pass the information on to your parent or parents.

If you have tried several of these methods and your needs still are not being met, you may want to speak to a school counselor. In some cases, parents can become easily overwhelmed and may not respond well to the extra stress and pressure involved in caring for a sick child. If you are being neglected—if you are being left alone overnight, if there is no food in the house—you will need to get help. This is when you definitely should speak to a guidance counselor or a school social worker.

Above all, an illness in the family changes the family dynamic. If your mother or father is sick, you may find yourself switching roles and acting like the parent at times while your parent may seem like the child. If it's your brother or sister who is sick, you might feel lonely or out of place. Maybe your older brother was always there to show you the ropes and now he is not able to. Or maybe your sibling is younger and you don't have him or her to follow you around and make you feel important. These changes can be confusing, and it will take some adjusting until you feel comfortable. The important thing is to give yourself time and to express how you feel.

CHAPTER THREE
DON'T NEGLECT YOURSELF

Depending on the severity of the illness, having a sick family member can seem all-consuming. Dealing with the emotions of shock or sadness can take a lot of energy. At the same time, there might be a lot of medical information being thrown at your family, which can be confusing to understand. Maybe there is a lot of back-and-forth travel to the hospital, or new routines to learn. It is an incredibly stressful time.

When someone in your family is ill, you may be on your own more than usual. You may have less access to your parents or other siblings since you will all be chipping in and trying to help out. In this case, you will have to be even more responsible than usual. If this is a scary thought, don't be alarmed. Remember that you are a very resourceful person.

After all, look at what you have been able to do while your parent, brother, sister, or other close relative has been out of commission. You have helped to organize how and when extra chores need to get done, and you have spoken up for yourself when you've needed information about your family member's illness or when you've wanted to remind your parent or parents that you need attention, too. All in all, you have been a great help to everyone.

DON'T NEGLECT YOURSELF | 27

Along with all the other things to take care of when your family member is sick, make sure you take care of yourself.

However, while you have been busy helping out and being mature, responsible, and a wonder-kid, you have to make certain that you are not neglecting yourself. It is important that during this tough time, you make sure you're in top shape so that no one has to worry about you on top of everything else. You also want to be strong so that you can be able to help anyone who needs you.

Here is an example of what one kid in your situation did to take care of himself.

LIVING WITH AN ILLNESS IN THE FAMILY

When my mother was sick, I was basically on my own because my dad isn't around. She was in the hospital and then she would come back home for a week or so, and then she would go back in for more tests. I had no relatives close-by, and since my mother wasn't working, we didn't have much money. I ended up getting food wherever I could—sometimes at a church and other times I'd go through the dumpster behind McDonald's. Eventually, I had to drop out of school and get a job so that we could pay the rent and keep our apartment. At the time, I was only fourteen, the best I could do was helping a landscaper in our town. But I was stressed out and I couldn't sleep. My mind would spin and I couldn't focus on anything. I needed to relax but I couldn't.

My track coach had always been nice to me, and he called to find out why I wasn't coming to school anymore. When I told him, he helped me fill out the forms for welfare so that I could quit the job and go back to school. He also told me about an afterschool program at the YMCA. I went there five days a week after school and got help with my homework, plus they had a lot of good programs. I met a lot of kids there who also didn't have a lot of money. They took turns inviting me over for dinner and to sleep over so I wouldn't be alone, or worse, so they wouldn't put me in a foster home. It went on like this for six months, and then my mother got better and she came back home for good. Life is still kind of hard, but whenever I get stressed out, I go for a run and all of my troubles seem to go away.

—Paul, sixteen, Fresno, CA

YOU CAN COPE WITH STRESS

Paul found that jogging was a good way of dealing with the stresses involved in having a sick parent. The thought of running may stress you out even more, but is there an activity you enjoy that relaxes you? Perhaps it's another sport. Maybe it's a craft or an art project. Perhaps you like reading books or talking on the phone to friends. Think of a few activities that you like and make

Sports can be a great way to take out your frustrations and get your mind off your troubles at home. You might also want to pursue an activity that calms and relaxes you.

sure that you allow yourself some time to do things that give you pleasure.

While some stress can be a good thing, too much stress is bad for you. Stress is useful when it motivates you to get things done. But it is bad if it is getting in the way of you being able to function normally.

How do you know if you are under too much stress? Take a look at the questions below. If you answer "yes" to most of the following questions, chances are that you need some help managing your stress.

- Are you having difficulty sleeping?
- Have you experienced any changes in appetite—either eating a lot more or a lot less than usual?
- Do you find that your mind is racing from idea to idea and you are unable to concentrate?
- Are you having trouble enjoying the things that you usually take pleasure in?
- Are you experiencing unusual stomach pains or headaches?
- Do you feel more irritable than usual?
- Have people remarked to you that you are acting strange or differently?

You may be wondering how you can ask for help when your whole family is in turmoil. If you don't feel that you can voice your concerns to a parent or older relative, try talking to your school counselor, a teacher, or the parent of a good friend. If you really do not know where to go for help, take a look on the Internet. There are a lot of resources available. You might even find an online support group you can turn to for help from the comfort of your home.

ONLINE SUPPORT GROUPS

You've finally realized you need help dealing with the stress of having a sick family member, but where are you supposed to turn? A counselor or therapist could help, but maybe you don't want to bother your parents, pay the expense, or figure out how to get there. You could talk to your guidance counselor, family friend, or youth leader at your church or temple, but maybe you're embarrassed or shy. Or maybe you don't have time, what with school, your homework, and extra work around the house.

An online support group could be your solution. Support groups can be especially helpful in a situation like yours, when you want someone to listen to your problems. In addition, since members will be going through the same or similar situations, they'll be able to understand you in ways your friends may not. They may have suggestions for coping with stress and other ways to get you through life's challenges.

When seeking an online support group, make sure you look for one that is associated with a reputable organization. As with all Internet use, remember to stay safe: Never give out any personal information like your address or where you like to hang out. Don't send any photos of yourself. The site should be moderated by an expert, and the people you talk to should be caring and supportive.

DON'T GET BEHIND AT SCHOOL

If you are going through a difficult time at home because of a family member's illness, you may want to notify your teacher of your current situation. Often an illness can get in the way of your having enough time to do homework. In addition, you might not be able to attend school every day. If this is the case, instead of keeping quiet while your grades drop and your teachers become annoyed with you for never being there, speak up. If you and your teachers work together, you will be able to make up an alternate schedule that will allow you to keep up with your classes. This is what Megan did.

> My mom had to take on two jobs because my stepdad had a heart attack and couldn't work. My mom needed me to stay at home a few days a week to look after my little sisters. Even though my mom told me to tell my teacher what was going on, I didn't because I was embarrassed. Also, my teacher was very strict and I thought she wouldn't care. I missed lots of school and got kicked off the soccer team.
> Then the principal called. My mom was the one who answered the phone, and she ended up spilling the beans. At first I was really mad at her, but Mr. Ross was surprisingly nice and he talked to my soccer coach and now I am back on the team and I am getting tutored so I can keep up with the rest of my classes.

No matter what you are going through at home, remember that school is important, too. Your teachers are there to help you learn, and most of the time, they will be understanding if you give them a chance and are open and honest with them.

Be honest with your teachers and let them know what's going on in your family. They want to help you succeed. Most likely, they can make special allowances to accommodate your situation.

Also, school can be a nice diversion from what's going on at home. Don't forget that you have your friends there who can be a great source of comfort and distraction when things are rough at home. Going to class and occupying your brain with learning will give you the chance to take your mind off feeling sad or worried.

When someone in your family becomes ill, it is easy to let certain things, like your schoolwork and your health, fall by the wayside. But remember that you need to make sure you are taking care of yourself. This means eating right, getting plenty of rest, keeping up with your schoolwork, and making time for friends. It will be hard to fit everything in if you've got extra responsibilities, and some things might suffer. But try to keep up as best you can.

Chapter four

WHEN HOPE RUNS OUT

Maybe it's the first thing you thought when you heard your family member was ill. Or maybe you haven't let yourself think that far ahead. But it might be necessary to confront the possibility that your family member's health will not improve.

If words such as "fatal" and "terminal" are being used to describe your sick family member, you may want to start thinking about the fact that he or she may not be around forever. The idea of death and long-term illness is never easy to come to terms with. When hope runs out and it appears that your loved one, be it your parent, grandparent, sibling, cousin, aunt, or uncle, may not get better, you need to start preparing yourself for the harsh and unpleasant reality of death.

Saying goodbye to a loved one, including a family pet, can be emotional and traumatic. Allow yourself the proper time to let them know how much they mean to you.

LIVING WITH AN ILLNESS IN THE FAMILY

In these situations, denial can be hard to overcome. How are you supposed to get your mind around the fact that someone whom you love dearly may never be the same again (in terms of terminal, debilitating illness), or may die soon? This resource does not attempt to provide any answers, but we would like to mention some things to keep in mind if you and your family find yourselves in this situation.

HOW TO SAY GOOD-BYE

Knowing someone with a terminal illness can be a long and exhausting experience. However, as the experts at Helpguide.org note, terminal illnesses allow loved ones the time to accept that their family member will die. This means there is time to tell the ill family member how much you have appreciated them, and to make amends for anything you feel guilty about.

Sometimes, terminally ill people don't let go of life because they sense that their loved ones aren't ready for them to go. Knowing that their family members are secure and able to carry on can offer a dying person tremendous relief.

If a loved one is terminally ill, make sure you take the time to say a proper good-bye. This can be during one visit or over the course of much time spent with the ill relative. Think about all this person has done for you, and remember all the good times you've shared and all you've learned from him or her. Some things you might say are "I love you," "Thank you," "You've taught me so much," "I'll never forget you," "I'll miss you so much," and "I'll be fine."

ACHIEVING CLOSURE

As you have learned, the importance of communication cannot be stressed enough. With fatal illness and death in the picture, it is even more vital that you keep the communication lines open. Saying good-bye to a loved one is hard; in fact, it's more than hard. It may be one of the most difficult things you do in your life. And though it may seem easier to deny that death is an unavoidable fact, don't do it. You will regret it later on. Instead, think of a way to say good-bye to your loved one. This will provide closure (a sense of completion), and that will help you go on with your life. Here are some examples of how kids your age were able to achieve closure.

Terminal or long-term illnesses allow you to achieve closure. You will have time to accept the loss of your loved one and to tell the person how much you appreciate him or her before your loved one is gone.

My cat was dying. We were going to put her to sleep in a week. I made sure we had nice photos of her, and I talked to her and told her how much I loved her. She had stopped purring a while ago, but the last time I picked her up, she purred. It was like she was saying good-bye to me, too. Now whenever I miss her, I look at her picture, and it's like she's still here.
—Masako, thirteen, Iowa City, IA

My sister got in a car crash. She went into a coma and the doctors said she wasn't going to come out. We didn't know how long my sister would live, but every time I went to visit her, before I left, I would always hold her hand and tell her she was my best friend. I did this every day for two months until the day she died. I'm glad I did it. It made it easier to let go.
—Aisha, fifteen, Sacramento, CA

My mother had a disease called multiple sclerosis. She got worse and worse for years. We never knew when we would lose her. It made no sense to me. I was mad, and I couldn't believe she would go away forever. My dad took me to see our priest. Father Joe told me to pray for my mother's soul so that God would hear me. Every night I said an extra prayer for my mom, and when she finally died, I put a photo of the two of us in her coffin. I know I'll always be with her and that God did what he thought was best.

—Rosaria, fourteen, Denver, CO

Lean on your family members when a loved one is sick or dying. They know you best, and they understand how you are feeling. Remember, you are in it together.

LIVING WITH AN ILLNESS IN THE FAMILY

Your family is one thing you can count on throughout life. Friends may come and go, but family will be there for you through the ups and downs. Going through the experience of having an ill family member is extremely challenging, and it may test the boundaries of your family. But if you remember to communicate your feelings, ask for help, and work together, it can also make your family stronger.

GLOSSARY

adrenaline Secretion of the adrenal glands, located above the kidneys, that causes a sudden increase in energy and physical strength.
betrayal The breaking of trust.
closure The act of ending or concluding something, physically or emotionally.
coma State of prolonged and deep unconsciousness, usually caused by a serious head injury.
denial Refusal to admit the truth, or being unable to deal with the reality of a situation.
fatal Deadly.
guilt Feelings of self-reproach for not behaving or acting in an appropriate way.
multiple sclerosis Disease of the nerve insulation in the brain and spinal cord.
neglect Uncared for.
reciprocate To do something in response to something another person has done, as in a favor.
regress To revert to a past type of behavior; in particular, going back to behavior patterns of one's youth.
resourceful Finding ways to cope with challenges.
sibling Brother or sister.
terminal illness A disease or other illness that cannot be cured and will most likely result in the eventual death of the afflicted.
vital Necessary to maintain life.

FOR MORE INFORMATION

Alex's Lemonade Stand Foundation
333 E. Lancaster Avenue, #414
Wynnewood, PA 19096
(610) 649-3034
Website: http://www.alexslemonade.org
Alex's Lemonade Stand raises money and awareness of childhood cancer causes, primarily research into new treatments and cures.

American Cancer Society
250 Williams Street NW
Atlanta, GA 30303
(800) 227-2345
Website: http://www.cancer.org
For more than 100 years, the American Cancer Society (ACS) has funded research with the goal of saving lives and creating a world with less cancer.

Big Brothers Big Sisters of America
P.O. Box 141599
Irving, TX 75014
(469) 351-3100
Website: http://www.bbbsa.org
Big Brothers Big Sisters makes meaningful, monitored matches between adult volunteers and children ages six through eighteen, in communities across the country.

Boys and Girls Club of Canada
2005 Sheppard Avenue E., Suite 400
Toronto, ON M2J 5B4
Canada
(905) 477-7272

FOR MORE INFORMATION | 43

Website: https://www.bgccan.com/EN/Pages/default.aspx
Boys and Girls Clubs of Canada provide safe, supportive places where youth can experience new opportunities, overcome barriers, build positive relationships, and develop confidence and skills for life.

Canadian Cancer Society
55 St Clair Avenue West
Suite 300
Toronto, ON M4V 2Y7
Canada
(416) 961-7223
Website: http://www.cancer.ca
The Canadian Cancer Society is a national, community-based organization of volunteers whose mission is the eradication of cancer and the enhancement of the quality of life of people living with cancer.

Canadian Red Cross Society
170 Metcalfe Street
Ottawa, ON K2P 2P2
Canada
(613) 740-1900
Website: http://www.redcross.ca
The Canadian Red Cross's mission is to improve the lives of vulnerable people by mobilizing the power of humanity in Canada and around the world.

Mental Health America
2000 N. Beauregard Street, 6th Floor
Alexandria, VA 22311
(703) 684-7722

Website: http://www.nmha.org
Mental Health America promotes mental health as a critical part of overall wellness, including prevention services for all, early identification and intervention for those at risk, and integrated care and treatment for those who need it, with recovery as the goal.

Starlight Children's Foundation
2049 Century Park East, Suite 4320
Los Angeles, CA 90067
(310) 479-1212
Website: http://www.starlight.org
Starlight Children's Foundation partners with experts to improve the life and health of kids and families around the world. The organization offers several programs for chronically ill children, teens, and their families.

WEBSITES

Because of the changing nature of Internet links, Rosen Publishing has developed an online list of websites related to the subject of this book. This site is updated regularly. Please use this link to access this list:

http://www.rosenlinks.com/FIY/Ill

FOR FURTHER READING

Barber, Nicola and Patience Coster. *Euthanasia*. London, England: Franklin Watts, 2012.

Chastain, Zachary and Camden Flath. *Sick All the Time*. Broomall, PA: Mason Crest Publishers, 2011.

Fields, Julianna. *Families Living with Mental and Physical Challenges*. Broomall, PA: Mason Crest Publishers, 2010.

Golden, Robert N. *The Truth About Illness and Disease*. New York, NY: Facts On File, 2010.

Heiney, Sue P. and Joan F. Hermann. *Cancer in Our Family*. Atlanta, GA: American Cancer Society, 2013.

Henningfield, Diane Andrews. *Death and Dying*. Farmington Hills, MI: Greenhaven Press, 2010.

Johnson, Leona. *Strengthening Family and Self*. Tinley Park, IL: Goodheart-Willcox Co., 2012.

Krementz, Jill. *How it Feels When a Parent Dies*. New York, NY: Knopf, 2010.

Libal, Autumn. *Chronic Illness*. Broomall, PA: Mason Crest, 2015.

McCue, Kathleen and Ron Bonn. *How to Help Children Through a Parent's Serious Illness*. New York, NY: St. Martin's Griffin, 2011.

Miles, Liz. *Coping with Illness*. Chicago, IL: Heinemann Library, 2011.

Owens, Jim and Bill Cass. *The Survivorship Net*. Atlanta, GA: American Cancer Society, 2010.

Thompson, Tamara. *The Right to Die*. Detroit, MI: Greenhaven Press, 2014.

INDEX

A

acceptance, 10
adrenaline, 17
anger, 9–10, 11, 13, 16–17, 20

C

chores/responsibilities, extra, 4, 16, 18–20, 26
closure, 37
communication, importance of, 15, 37
confusion, 8, 11, 12, 13, 16, 25
crying, 10

D

death, 35, 37
denial, 7–8, 10–11, 36, 37

E

emotion diary, 10–11

F

fatal/terminal illness, 35, 36, 37
fear, 4, 11, 15

G

good-bye, saying, 36, 37
guilt, 10, 11, 21

H

help, asking for, 18, 30
homework, 32, 34
hotlines, 9

K

knowledge, as power, 14–15

L

loneliness, 4, 10, 20

N

notes, writing, 23–24

O

online support, 30, 31

R

regression, 22, 23
research, 14
resentment, 20

S

sadness, 4, 10, 26
school, 21, 32–34
school counselors, 9, 15, 24, 25, 30
shock, 6, 26
siblings, when they are sick, 20–25
social workers, 8, 9, 25
stress, 4, 15, 19, 21, 24, 31
    coping with, 29–30

46

T

Task Hat, 20
teachers, talking to, 9, 14, 30, 32
terminal/fatal illness, 35, 36, 37

W

writing down your emotions, 10–11

ABOUT THE AUTHORS

Viola Jones is a writer and middle school teacher. As a child, she loved to raise the spirits of her chronically ill grandmother.

Tabitha Wainwright has a degree in education as well as a master's degree in children's literature.

PHOTO CREDITS

Cover (figure) ostill/Shutterstock.com; cover (background), p. 1 clockwise from top left XiXinXing/Shutterstock.com, Photographee.eu/Shutterstock.com (top and bottom right), Iakov Filimonov/Shutterstock.com; p. 3 sezer66/Shutterstock.com; pp. 4-5, 24 ERproductions Ltd/Blend Images/Getty Images; pp. 6, 16, 26, 35 (top) XiXinXing/Shutterstock.com; p. 7 Comstock Images/Stockbyte/Thinkstock; pp. 8-9 Richard Clark/E+/Getty Images; p. 14 Jupiterimages/Pixland/Thinkstock; p. 17 © Jaime Monfort/Moment/Getty Images; p. 19 Fuse/Thinkstock; p. 27 JGI/Jamie Grill/Blend Images/Getty Images; p. 29 Tony Garcia/Image Source/Getty Images; p. 33 Chris Schmidt/E+/Getty Images; p. 35 Vstock/Getty Images; p. 37 RubberBall Productions/Brand X Pictures/Getty Images; pp. 38-39 Jani Bryson/iStock/Thinkstock; cover and interior pages patterns and textures Irina_QQQ/Shutterstock.com, ilolab/Shutterstock.com, Cluckv/Shutterstock.com, phyZick/Shutterstock.com; back cover Anna-Julia/Shutterstock.com

Designer: Michael Moy; Editor: Christine Poolos;
Photo Researcher: Karen Huang